THE ENCHANTED LAKE

THE
ENCHANTED LAKE

CLASSIC IRISH FAIRY STORIES

SINÉAD DE VALERA

CURRACH
PRESS

First published in 2005 by
CURRACH PRESS
55A Spruce Avenue, Stillorgan Industrial Park, Blackrock,
Co Dublin, Ireland

www.currach.ie

1 3 5 4 2

Cover design and cover illustration by Daniel Gaynor
Illustrations by Tana French
Origination by Currach Press
Printed by Betaprint Ltd, Dublin

ISBN 1-85607-923-6

CONTENTS

THE THREE DRINKS

It is many centuries since the beautiful Lady Ina lived in a splendid castle near the banks of the Shannon in the centre of Ireland. Her parents had died when she was a little child and, though she was still young, she had full control over all her possessions. She was proud of her wealth and beauty. Many suitors sought her hand but she refused them all. At last she had a notice sent out that she would marry the man whose singing she most liked. Numbers of singers came to the castle but all failed to please the haughty beauty.

In a small house some distance from the castle there lived a widow named Brigid with her three sons, Cathal, Fionn and Dermot. The family was poor, for the elder boys never did any work. Cathal was a terrible sleepyhead.

He lay in bed till very late in the day and after he got up, he moped about the house and was useless and idle. Fionn was bright and lively but he was always looking for amusement. He spent most of his time playing and seeking sport. All the work was left to the mother and Dermot. They toiled day and night.

All four were taking their midday meal one cold day in March when an old woman came to the door. Brigid welcomed the stranger and placed food before her.

'I think you have never been here before,' said Brigid.

'No,' said the woman, 'my home is on the other side of the river but I know a good deal about the people here.'

'Will you tell us your name?' asked Brigid.

'Eavan is my name.'

When the meal was over, the stranger sat down at the fire and began to sing in a low, crooning voice. The mother and sons listened with curiosity to the words:

'Fair is Ina to behold,
Proud her heart and hard and cold,
She must learn through grief and pain
Love she scorned to find again.'

When Eavan had finished the verse she sat for a while in silence, gazing into the fire. Then she began to sing again.

'Of the brothers only one,
E'er has been a loving son.
Joy and gladness on him wait,
Others will be wise too late.'

When she had finished the song she rose to depart.

'You have a kind heart,' she said to Brigid, 'but I see you are poor.'

'Indeed, we are poor,' said Brigid, 'and my sons have hardly enough to eat.'

'Will the eldest come with me? I will make him rich and happy, if he does what I tell him.'

Cathal was delighted at the idea of becoming rich and said he would gladly go. He set out with the old woman and was surprised to find how quickly she could walk. In fact, he could hardly keep pace with her. They reached the side of the river where a strange-looking boat with a large green sail awaited them. When they got into the boat, it skimmed over the water and in a moment it had reached the other side of the river.

Eavan then led Cathal through a wood, at the far end of which was a large field. A little house stood in a corner of the field. Near the house there were hens and ducks and at one side a number of pigs were rooting in the earth. Some cows and a large brown goat were grazing in the centre of the field. Eavan brought Cathal into the house and gave him a good meal.

'There is a comfortable bed in here,' she said, as she opened the door of a small room. 'You can rest there for the night. I am going away early in the morning and will not be back till tomorrow night. I will call you when I am leaving, for you will have a big day's work before you.'

'And what will be my reward?' asked Cathal, who did not like the idea of doing hard work.

'You will get a rich reward if you do your work well. You have heard of the Lady Ina.'

'Yes,' said Cathal. 'I have heard she will marry the man whose singing most pleases her.'

'That is true,' said Eavan, 'and of course

her husband will be very rich, for she has great wealth. Now, I can prepare a drink which will give you a beautiful voice and will also enable you to compose a song that will charm the Lady Ina's heart.'

'That is a great reward,' said Cathal.

'That reward will be yours, if everything is in order here on my return. First you must go to the far end of the woods where the driest sticks are and bring home as many as you can carry. When you have lit the fire, you will go down to the well at the end of the field for a pitcher of water. When you have had your breakfast, you will put on the fire a big pot of food for the pigs. Then you must milk the cows and feed the poultry. You must prepare your own dinner and bring home some more firewood. In the evening you will again do the milking and feeding of the animals. Be careful to shut the hen house, for the fox is sure to be prowling about. Now, go to bed. I hope you will sleep soundly till I call you.'

Next morning at dawn the old woman called Cathal.

'Get up at once,' she said. 'It is a bitterly

cold morning and the poor animals will want their food. I am leaving now.'

She walked down the little stony path that led from the house. Cathal waited till the sound of her footsteps had died away and then turned over and went asleep again.

'What a fool I am,' said he, as he closed his eyes, 'to get up so early on a cold morning like this.'

He lay in bed till it was quite late but as he began to feel hungry he got up and went to the woods. The cold March wind made him shiver and it was a long time before he succeeded in lighting the fire. He went to the well and brought back the water. It was past midday when he had his breakfast ready.

'I won't bother milking till evening,' he thought to himself, 'and the old woman will never know if I do not feed the fowl nor the pigs. I will just open the sty and the hen house and take a little rest till dinnertime. I am very tired after all the hard work I have done.'

He sat down at the fire and let the time slip by till he was hungry again. He prepared another meal. By the time he had eaten it, darkness was coming on. The fire was going out, for he had burned all the sticks he had brought from the woods.

'Indeed,' said he to himself, 'the animals can look after themselves. I am not going out in the cold and if I sit here without a fire, I will perish. I will go to bed and get a good sleep.'

He did not even close the hen house nor the pig sty.

Later on, when the moon was shining brightly, the old woman returned. She heard the poor cows lowing and the pigs grunting with all their might. Just as she came near the house, she saw the fox running away with a fine, fat hen in his mouth. Now, the brown goat was really a fairy goat and had the power of speech. She told the old woman that Cathal had not milked the cows nor fed the fowl nor pigs.

When Eavan went into the house all was cold and dark. From the room came the sound of loud snoring.

'Very well, Cathal, my boy, you will get a rich reward in the morning,' she said to herself.

When morning came Eavan said nothing to Cathal about the work she had left him to do.

'You may go now,' she said, 'after I have prepared a drink for you.'

She went out and milked the goat and gathered some herbs. When she came back into the house, she mixed the herbs in a vessel with the milk. As she did so, Cathal noticed that she smiled and chuckled to herself. When Cathal had taken the drink, Eavan said to him:

'Go now to the riverside. The boat will be waiting for you. Go then to the Lady Ina's castle. Say you wish to sing for her and wait for the result. She has given directions that all singers of every description are to be admitted.'

Cathal started off in high glee. When he reached the castle he was admitted at once into the presence of the Lady Ina. She and Róisín, her favourite attendant, were sitting on gold chairs on a raised platform. Numbers of other attendants were present.

'Your name?' said Ina.

'Cathal is my name, my lady.'

'Begin your song.'

Cathal opened his mouth but instead of singing he burst into peals of laughter. He laughed and laughed and shook with laughter until everyone in the room except Ina herself was laughing with him.

'Call the strongest men in the castle,' she said, 'and have this madman carried out.'

Four great big men came in. One caught hold of Cathal's right arm, another of his left. The other two grasped his feet. Cathal continued to roar laughing all the time, such was the power of the drink the old woman had given him. The four men carried him from the castle and threw him on the ground outside the gates. He got up slowly and went home. He was ashamed of himself and told his mother he would go away in the morning to seek his fortune, for he now knew he must work if he wished to become rich. He fell asleep that night tittering and chuckling but in the morning the effects of the draught had worn away and he set out on his travels.

A couple of days after this, the old woman came again to Brigid's house. This time she took Fionn home with her. She gave him the same instructions that she had given Cathal. She promised him the same reward and wakened him when she was going out in the morning. Fionn got up and went to the woods. He gathered the sticks and hurried back, but just as he came in sight of the house he heard voices in the next field. He dropped the sticks and went through the hedge. Some boys were running up and down the field as if they were practising for a race.

'Will you let me run with you?' he asked. For a long time he paced and ran through the field with the boys until he began to feel hungry. He gathered up the sticks and hurried back to the house. After having lighted the fire, he went to the well for the water. By the time he had breakfast over, it was past eleven o'clock.

'Oh dear,' thought he, 'I must hurry and milk the cows and feed the fowl! I can prepare the pigs' food when I come back.'

When he went out to milk, the first thing that caught his eye was a kite entangled in the branches of a high tree at the side of the field. Some boys had been flying the kite and they were trying to get it down from the tree. Fionn dropped the milking pail and ran to help the boys. They soon succeeded in loosening the kite. Fionn could not resist the delight of flying and following it. In this manner another few hours passed away. He began to feel uneasy and as he returned to the house he decided he would not milk the cows nor goat till evening. As for the poultry and pigs, he would not open either hen house or sty and then the old woman would think that he had fastened up both places for the night. He prepared another meal for himself and was just finishing it when he heard the sound of music. The sound came from a distance. Fionn ran to the place from whence it came. At the crossroads he saw a fiddler and with him a number of boys and girls who were dancing to his music. He joined the dance and continued to enjoy himself until darkness came on.

In the meantime, the old woman returned home. She heard the lowing of the cows and the goat ran to meet her.

'None of your commands have been obeyed,' said the goat. 'The hen house and pig sty have not been opened all day and the cows have not been milked.'

When Eavan went into the house, she found everything cheerless and dark. In a short time Fionn came back, puffing and panting.

'You can go to bed now,' said the old woman in a quiet voice, 'and I will prepare a drink for you in the morning.' She went out early the next day, milked the goat and gathered some herbs. As she mixed the herbs in the milk she shed many tears.

'There must be plenty of onions in that drink,' thought Fionn. When he had taken the mixture, Eavan gave him the same directions that she had given Cathal.

Fionn was shown into Ina's presence.

'Your name?' said she.

'Fionn is my name, my lady.'

'Begin your song.'

Fionn squared his shoulders and cleared his throat to begin to sing, but instead of a song, sighs and sobs choked his voice and he burst out crying. He wept and wept until two of the attendants brought in a vessel to catch the tears.

Ina stood up in a rage. 'Call the men to remove this weeping fool,' she ordered.

Fionn, weeping and wailing, was carried out. He went home.

'I see now, Mother,' he said, 'that though fun is a good and pleasant thing, we cannot have it all the time and we must work if we are to be rich and happy.'

Even in his sleep he was sobbing and sighing but towards morning the effects of the drink passed away. Like his brother Cathal, he left home and went to seek his fortune.

Some days later the old woman again came to Brigid's house.

'Will you let your youngest son come with me?' she asked.

'I would be very lonely without him,' said the poor mother.

'Let me try my luck, Mother,' said Dermot. 'Whether I succeed or fail, I will come back to you.'

The mother consented. The woman took Dermot to her house. She gave him the same directions that she had given to his brothers.

When she called him in the morning, he

jumped out of bed. He got the wood for the fire, the water from the well and did everything the woman had told him to do. When she returned at night the fire was burning brightly, the house was tidy and clean, the cows and goat had been milked and the pigs and poultry comfortably settled for the night. Everything was in perfect order.

Eavan smiled kindly. She told Dermot to go to bed and she would prepare the drink for him in the morning. Next morning, as she mixed the herbs and milk, Dermot heard her singing in a sweet, low voice:

'The magic of song,
Will soften e'er long,
The heart now so proud and cold.'

When Dermot had taken the drink, he thanked Eavan and set out for the castle. As he entered the room where Ina was, he thought how beautiful she was and how much he would like to have her for his wife.

Róisín, Ina's friend, whispered in her ear, 'I like his face.'

'Don't mind his face,' said Ina haughtily,

'Of all the singers that have come, you are the one
that has pleased me most.'

'I want to hear his voice.'

'Your name?' she said to Dermot.

'Dermot is my name.'

'Let me hear you sing.'

Ina listened with rapt attention as Dermot sang the following words to the air for which – ages after – Moore wrote the song, 'No not more welcome the fairy numbers':

'Oh, noble lady, your worth and beauty
Stir in my bosom affection true.
Will you accept all the love and duty
I offer to you with homage due?
Oh, see me here, so humbly kneeling.
Turn not from me in your pride,
But hear my song with its soft appealing
That I may claim you for my sweet bride.'

The tears were in Ina's eyes as she called Dermot toward her at the end of the song. Then she looked at his poor clothes.

'Of all the singers that have come,' she said, 'you are the one that has pleased me most; but I could not marry a poor, shabby man like you.'

'Oh, my lady!' said Róisín. 'You cannot break your word.'

'Silence,' said Ina. 'I am mistress here and I can do as I wish.'

Dermot bowed to Ina and walked in silence from the room. He could not help thinking of her beautiful face and he wished his song had softened her heart. When he reached his mother's house, whom should he find there but Eavan.

'Well,' said she, 'what is your news?'

Dermot told her all that had happened.

'The proud beauty will be sorry for what she has done,' said Eavan, 'and good fortune will come to you, if you do as I tell you.' She then gave Dermot a suit of fine clothes and told him to put it on.

'Now take this purse of gold,' she said. 'Go away and travel through the country. Your beautiful voice will make you great and famous and you will be welcome in the wealthiest houses. Come back after a year and a day. I shall be waiting for you here in your mother's house.'

Brigid said goodbye to her son and he set off on his travels.

After Ina had sent Dermot away, she became very sad and unhappy. She was ashamed, too, that she had broken her word. Her wealth seemed useless and she felt she would willingly part with it all, if by so doing she could bring Dermot back again.

One day nearly a year after his departure, Róisín found Ina sitting by the bank of a stream which flowed through the castle grounds. She was crying bitterly.

'What is the cause of your grief, my lady?' Róisín asked.

'Oh, Róisín, I have been very unhappy since I sent Dermot away! His song is ever in my ears. I wish he would come back again.'

'I fear, my lady, he will not come back. He went away from home the day he left the castle.'

'It was I that sent him away and now I know I would rather marry him than any other man in the world.'

Neither Ina nor Róisín had noticed that Eavan stood behind them as they talked.

'Go back to the castle now, Róisín,' said Ina.

When Eavan heard this she hurried away. Her swift walking brought her to the castle gates some time before Róisín reached them. Eavan stopped Róisín as she was about to enter the castle.

'Do you wish the Lady Ina to be happy again?'

'Oh, indeed I do!'

'Then do as I tell you. A year and a day from the time Dermot left home, bring Ina to his mother's house at nightfall. Tell her she will hear news of him if she goes there. Say nothing to her till the day comes. If you do as I say, she will be happy.' Having said these words, Eavan walked quietly away.

Early on the day on which Dermot was to return home, Eavan went to Brigid's house. At midday Dermot himself arrived. He rode a fine horse and his clothes were so magnificent that his mother hardly knew him. He had become rich and famous. Towards evening Eavan told him to put on the old clothes he had worn before he went away. He wondered at this request, but he knew Eavan was a friend and he did as she said.

As the darkness was coming on, Eavan went to the door and kept looking out. At last she asked Dermot to sing the song he had sung for Ina. Again Dermot wondered at the strange request, but he did as Eavan asked. At the close of the song a wonderful thing happened. Eavan moved from the door and Ina, followed by Róisín, came quickly in and knelt down beside Dermot.

'Oh, will you forgive me?' she cried. 'I have never ceased to regret the wrong I have done. I will be your wife if you still wish to marry me.'

'But look at his shabby clothes,' said Eavan.

'His clothes do not matter,' said Ina. 'I would rather marry him than marry the richest man in the world.'

'Now, Dermot,' said Eavan, 'tell the Lady Ina how it has fared with you since she sent you away.'

When Ina heard of the power and wealth which Dermot had gained, she feared he would not want her for his wife, but he forgave her and they were married almost immediately. The wedding feast lasted for many days and the last day was better than the first. Eavan was the principal guest at the wedding and was afterwards a constant visitor at the happy home. Ina became so kind and gentle that she was beloved not only by those in her own household but by everyone in the country round.

THE CAPTIVE PRINCESS

Years and years and years ago, when Fionn MacCool in Erin and Fionn Gall, a brother giant in Scotland, were building the Giant's Causeway, which was to run between the two countries, there lived in a glen in Antrim a young man named Hugh.

Everyone liked Hugh. He was very kind and neighbourly and it made him sad to see anyone in pain or trouble. He had also a great love for animals.

All the people in the place where Hugh lived had heard of an unhappy princess who had been carried off by a wicked giant and was kept a captive in his castle. This castle was a *crannóg* or lake dwelling. It was built on stakes of wood driven down deep in the earth in the centre of the lake. The giant's

28

wife was a witch and if anyone attempted to cross the lake, she set the water in motion and caused it to form whirlpools so that neither swimmer nor boat could reach the castle.

Hugh had a great desire to rescue the princess, whose name was Maca. One day he was sitting in his little house when he heard a wailing sound outside. He went to the door and saw a dog limping by, whining pitifully. He brought the dog into his house and saw that there was a large thorn in one of his front paws. He extracted the thorn and bathed the paw. The dog tried to thank him by licking his hand and then seemed to show that he wished Hugh to follow him. He led him some distance from his house and then turned down a narrow lane with high hedges on each side. At the end of the lane was a tiny little house. An old woman was sitting at the door. She looked very sad but when she saw the dog her face brightened. She thought he had been lost, he was so long away from her. The dog ran forward and put his head in her lap.

'I found this dog outside my house,' said

Hugh. 'There was a thorn in his paw and when I took it out, he seemed to wish me to follow him.'

'Good man,' said the old woman, 'and good dog. He wants me to befriend you as you have befriended him.'

Now this old woman was a *bean feasa* (a woman of knowledge), that is, a woman with magic powers and with knowledge of things distant and hidden. She talked with Hugh for some time and he told her of his desire to rescue the princess.

'It is a hard task,' said the old woman, 'and there are many dangers in the way, but you are strong and brave and you will succeed if you follow my directions.'

She went into the house and came out again with a large shell in her hand. Stretched across the shell were silver cords, something like the strings of a lute or violin. The old woman touched the strings and Hugh thought the music was the sweetest he had ever heard.

'Take this shell,' said the old woman. 'You will come to the Valley of Weasels. They will rush to swarm around and attack you, but touch the strings lightly and they will become harmless. You will then come to a dark, dense wood through which it will be impossible to pass. Again, touch the strings and all will be well. Next, you must cross a deep, rugged quarry, but at the sound of the music your way will be clear. You have a long journey before you and you will need food.'

Again she went into the house. She returned carrying a large oat cake.

'Take this,' she said, 'and my blessing with it.'

'I shall never forget your kindness,' said Hugh, as he set off with a stout heart.

It was not long before he reached the valley of weasels. They rushed towards him as if they would spring at his throat. Hugh drew his fingers across the strings of the shell. Immediately the weasels formed a line on each side of him and as he continued to play, they marched along with him till he passed out of the valley.

Next he came to the wood. The trees were so high and so close together that it was impossible for him to pass through. Hugh sounded the strings and all at once the branches parted and the trees themselves seemed to follow him till he came to the far end of the wood.

At last he reached the quarry. There were great, jagged rocks on each side and a hollow in the middle. When he began to play, the stones from the bottom rose up and formed a smooth path for him and those at the sides moved gently with him till he reached the farther end.

He now sat down to rest near a clump of sloe bushes. As he was eating his oat cake, a tiny little bird fell from a robin's nest in the bush. He rose at once and gently placed the fledgling back in the nest.

Suddenly a little man stood before him. He had bright, twinkling eyes and a very friendly smile. He handed Hugh a feather, saying as he did so:

'For this your kindly deed,
As on your way you speed,
Take this and in your need
'Twill serve you well.

'By the side of the water which surrounds the giant's castle you will see a seagull. Strike the bird with this feather.

'Now haste away,
Make no delay,
E'er close of day,
All will be well.'

Having said this, the little man vanished.

Hugh continued his journey. After a time he again sat down to rest and eat some more of the cake. Just above him was an old oak tree with ivy climbing along the trunk. A bat had in some strange way got entangled in the ivy and could not move and there it remained, with the glaring sunshine hurting its poor eyes. Hugh climbed up the tree and placed the bat on the shady side, hidden by the ivy and protected by the branches of the oak.

Again he heard the words:

'For this your kindly deed,
As on your way you speed,
Take this and in your need,
'Twill serve you well.'

There stood the little man, handing Hugh a bat's wing. 'If you turn this round three times in your right hand, darkness thick as night will fall about you. This darkness will last for a short time only.

'Now haste away,
Make no delay,
E'er close of day,
All will be well.'

Like a flash the little man was gone.

When Hugh had travelled for some time, he sat down on a stone by the roadside. From the other side of the hedge came a sound as if some creature were in pain. He went through the hedge to the place from which the sound came. There he saw a cat down in a deep well and unable to climb out. Hugh took off his coat and, leaning over the edge of the wall, lowered it towards the cat. Puss caught it with her forepaws and Hugh dragged her to safety.

'For this your kindly deed,
As on your way you speed,
Take this and in your need,
'Twill serve you well.'

There stood the little man, handing Hugh a

cat's eye. 'Take this,' he said, 'and if you hold it in front of you, the darkest way will become bright and clear before you.

'Now haste away,
Make no delay,
E'er close of day,
All will be well.'

Again the little man disappeared.

Hugh journeyed on. After a time he came in sight of a huge stone castle built in the centre of a lake. This he knew to be the giant's home. At one of the top windows he caught sight of a beautiful, sad face and he knew that the Princess Maca was a captive there.

As Hugh came near the castle he saw the giant and his wife standing on the steps. When the pair saw Hugh, the giant waved his club round his head and the woman raised her wand over the water. Immediately it foamed and turned in all directions and formed whirlpools all round the castle.

Hugh felt it would be impossible to cross that dangerous lake but just then he saw perched on the bank beside him a beautiful

All the people in the place where Hugh lived had heard of an unhappy princess who had been carried off by a wicked giant and was kept a captive in his castle.

seagull. Remembering the little man's advice, he struck the seagull with the feather. All at once the bird became so large and strong that Hugh mounted on its back and was carried across to the castle. When he descended from the back of the bird it flew up into the air.

The giant and his wife rushed down the steps but Hugh waved the bat's wing and in the darkness the pair lost their footing and fell headlong into the water. The whirlpools dragged them down, down and they were never heard of again.

By the light from the cat's eye, Hugh ascended the stairs to the room where the Princess Maca was. As he reached the door, the darkness disappeared and Hugh turned the key which was on the outside of the lock.

Maca told him she was the daughter of the King of Ulster.

'My father,' said she, 'banished from his kingdom a wicked giant. The giant's brother in revenge seized me and kept me imprisoned here.'

'But,' said Hugh, 'how could the giant take you from your father's home? Are there not guards and attendants there?'

'Yes,' said Maca, 'but the giant found out that I liked to walk alone in a lovely wood which is near the palace. One spring day as I was gathering violets, he came and bore me away so quickly that I could not even call for help.'

'Where is your father's castle?' Hugh asked.

'It is near the western coast and is so far away that I fear I shall never see my home again.'

Hugh led the princess down to the water's edge. There stood the seagull. Hugh touched it with the feather. As he did so it grew so large that he and Maca were able to mount on its back. It flew westwards over lakes and plains, over hills and valleys, till it reached a beautiful glen in the midst of the blue hills of Donegal.

There stood the castle before them, its windows shining like gold in the rays of the setting sun.

They dismounted from the seagull and the bird flew swiftly away.

No words can describe the joy of the king

and queen when they saw their daughter again. Maca told her parents all about her escape from the giant's castle and of Hugh's kindness and courage.

'You are a brave man,' said the king, 'and I should like to make you one of the chieftains of the kingdom.'

'That would be a great honor,' said Hugh, 'and nothing would please me better except something which is almost too good to ask for.'

'I know what that is,' said the queen. 'It is our daughter's hand in marriage.'

Hugh looked at Maca.

She placed her hand in his, saying, 'As I have already given you my heart, you may now take my hand.'

The happy pair were married amid scenes of great rejoicing and lived happily ever after.

THE HARE OF SLEEVEBAWN

Once upon a time there lived in a little house at the foot of the Wicklow Mountains a widow with her two sons, Feilim and Art. Feilim was a smart, clever boy who could learn very quickly, but poor Art was slow and shy and was sometimes spoken of as the *amadán* or fool. Feilim often joined with others in calling his brother stupid and awkward, but the mother always said that Art would yet be an intelligent and successful man. He had a kind heart and he tried to help with the farm work while his brother was out playing or idling about the place. Things went on like this till Feilim and Art had grown to be young men.

One lovely summer day Feilim took his

dog with him and wandered away from home till he came towards the mountain called Sleevebawn. He crossed over on the stepping stones of a stream and reached the foot of the mountain. There he lay down on the soft, green grass and watched the water hurrying down over the stones and pebbles on its way to the sea.

After a while he heard a rustle among the fern on the mountainside. Suddenly a large hare appeared and remained still for a moment. Feilim hurled his stick at the animal and hit it on the ear. It ran like lightning down the mountain and disappeared. Feilim marvelled at its size and speed. He urged his dog to follow it, but the animal whined and lay down at his feet.

Feilim returned home and told his mother what he had seen.

'Oh!' said the mother, 'that is the fairy hare of Sleevebawn. It is a hare by day but at night it takes the form of an ugly old hag. She lives in a cave at the foot of the mountain facing the sea. She is very fierce and no one has yet had courage to go near her, though some people say that there is great good fortune in store for anyone who would be brave enough to go and talk to her.'

Both Feilim and Art listened with great attention to what their mother had told them.

'Now,' thought Feilim, 'I shall be rich for life. I shall never have to work and shall always have a good time. I am clever and courageous and I will go to the cave and talk to the hag. She is sure to tell a fine handsome fellow like me where the treasure is to be found.'

He waited that night till the moon was high in the sky and then took his way to Sleevebawn. When he reached the stream he saw an old woman standing by the side of the water. She wished to cross the stream, but feared she would lose her footing on the stepping stones.

When she saw Feilim she said:

'Young stranger, kindly lend your aid,
To cross the stones I am afraid.'

'Get out of my way, old creature,' said Feilim, as he sprang across the stones and left the poor old woman standing there alone and sad.

He went down a sloping path towards the sea and came to a cave under the rocks. All at once he heard from inside the cave a harsh voice calling out:

'Who dares to come,
To my cavern home?'

Just then, out of the mouth of the cave came an ugly old woman with long teeth and piercing eyes. Feilim noticed that there was a piece out of the top of her left ear. As he looked into the cave he saw a number of lizards and toads there.

'I came,' said Feilim, 'to seek the wealth and good fortune that are to be found here.'

'Look at my ear,' said the hag, 'and think do you deserve either wealth or good fortune?'

'I am very sorry for any injury I have done you,' said Feilim.

'So you should be. It was a shame for you to ill-treat a harmless hare. However, now that you have dared to come to the cave, I may tell you there is hidden good fortune here for anyone who is brave enough and lucky enough to find it. The good fortune can be obtained only by one who will perform three difficult tasks which I will set him.'

'I will undertake to do any task, no matter how difficult it is,' said Feilim.

'Very well,' said the hag, 'but if you agree to do one of the tasks, you must attempt the three.'

'I am willing to attempt the three.'

'Here is the first,' said the hag. 'Take this basket of eggs. Go to the summit of Sleevebawn. Place the basket on your head. Put your hands behind your back and run down the mountainside without breaking one egg.'

Feilim did as the hag told him but when he attempted to run down the side of the mountain the basket fell down over his face and clothes so that he was all covered with egg yolks and whites.

'Hah! Hah!' the hag laughed. 'You have failed in your first task. Now try the second. Here is a tumbler without a bottom. Take a drink out of it from that large vessel of water on the floor.'

Feilim stooped to try to get a drink from the bottomless tumbler, but he succeeded only in wetting his clothes and mixing the water with the eggs.

The hag laughed again and said, 'You have failed in the second task, now for the third.'

She took the tongs and placed it in a fire which was at the far end of the cave. When it was red hot, she asked Feilim to take it and hold it in his hand till she told him to drop it.

Feilim caught told of the tongs but of course he dropped it immediately.

'Be gone,' said the hag, 'and never set foot near this place again.'

Feilim returned home. Next morning he told his mother he was tired of his life on the farm and that he would go away to seek his fortune. He did not say anything to her or to Art of his visit to the hag's cave.

Now, Art wished to make his mother rich and happy, for she was poor and had few of the comforts of life. About a month after Feilim's departure, he set out one fine morning for Sleevebawn. He hoped to have a chance of finding the hidden treasure.

Just as he had crossed the stream, the hare appeared from among the fern. For a moment it stood still. Then it sped down the mountain and was lost to sight.

'Poor hare,' said Art, 'may the fox never catch you.'

He went home and got through the day's work. When nightfall came he again took his way to Sleevebawn. The moon was shining brightly.

When he reached the stream he saw the old woman standing beside it.

She turned to him and said:

'Young stranger, kindly lend your aid,
To cross the stream I am afraid.'

'I'll help you across and welcome,' said Art, as he lifted the old woman in his strong arms and carried her safely over the slippery stones.

'Now,' said the old woman, 'I know you are going to the hag's cave to seek your fortune. She will set you three difficult tasks. For the first one take this little pad and place it on your head. Take this tumbler for the second and this iron glove for the third. Now leave me and may good luck go with you.'

Art went down the sloping path and came to the cave. As he approached he heard the harsh voice of the hag calling out:

'Who dares to come,
To my cavern home?'

He looked into the cave as the hag came towards him. Inside, amidst the dirt and slime, he saw a number of lizards and toads.

'Why do you come here?' asked the hag.

'I came,' said Art, 'to seek the good fortune that is to be found in this place. Tell me please what I must do to deserve the good fortune.'

'There are three tasks which you must perform,' said the hag, 'and I must warn you that if you agree to do one, you must attempt all three.'

'I promise to try any three tasks you set me,' said Art.

'Very well,' said the hag, 'first, take this basket of eggs. Climb to the top of Sleevebawn. Put the basket on your head.

Put your hands behind your back and run down the mountainside without breaking one of the eggs.'

Art took the basket and went up the mountain. He put the pad on his head, then placed the basket on it and ran down the mountainside without breaking an egg.

'Good man,' said the hag, 'you have succeeded in performing the first task. Now for the second. Here is a bottomless tumbler. There is water in that vessel on the floor. Take a drink of the water out of the tumbler.'

Art slipped into the bottomless tumbler the one which the old woman had given him. He stooped down, filled the tumbler and took a drink.

'Good again,' said the hag. 'Now for the third task.'

She put the tongs into the fire and waited till it was red hot.

'Now lift out the tongs and hold it in your hand till I tell you to drop it.'

Art slipped on the iron glove and lifted the tongs out of the fire. As he did so, a sort of faintness came over him and for a moment all was darkness.

When the light reappeared the cave was no longer there. In its stead was a magnificent castle and standing by his side was a beautiful girl and with her the old woman he had seen at the stream. Numbers of beautifully dressed men and women were there also.

Art rubbed his eyes to assure himself he was not dreaming.

Then the girl spoke.

'Thank you,' she said, 'for breaking the cruel spell that bound me. I am the daughter of a king and this is my fairy godmother.'

Art stared at the princess, but remembering his manners, bowed low to the ground.

'My attendants here,' continued the princess, 'were the toads and lizards you saw in the cave. The toads were the ladies and the lizards the gentlemen.'

'But, Your Highness,' said Art, 'where has the cave gone and what has brought about this wonderful change?'

'It is a long, sad story,' said the princess. 'I

When the light reappeared the cave was no longer there. In its stead was a magnificent castle and standing by his side was a beautiful girl.

shall ask my fairy godmother to tell it to you.'

'Her Highness,' said the fairy godmother, 'had the misfortune to lose her mother when she was very young. The king did not long survive the queen and the princess was put in the charge of an uncle. This uncle was a cruel, wicked man who wanted the kingdom for himself. He was afraid to have the princess killed but he sent for a cunning, evil witch who lived at some miles distance from his home, and promised her a large share of the wealth of the kingdom if she would get rid of the princess.

'"I will do that," said the witch, "if you will allow me to destroy the castle in which the princess is living at present."

'"There are many other castles in the kingdom," said the uncle, "and I am willing that this one should be destroyed, if only the princess can be got out of my way."

'The witch then used her evil powers and changed the castle into a cave and the ladies of the court into toads and the gentlemen into lizards.

'The poor princess herself became an

ugly, old hag. Even her voice and her whole nature were changed. She was as you have seen her, a harsh, rough-spoken, fierce woman. She was never allowed to leave the cave except for a short time in the day and then she had to take the form of a hare.'

The princess herself now spoke.

'The witch had no power over my fairy godmother. It was she who was able to lessen the spell. No evil spell can hold out forever against goodness and courage. My godmother knew that if she could find a kind, brave man who would perform the three difficult tasks which you have done, the spell would be broken.'

'But,' said Art, 'won't the cruel uncle find out that the spell is broken?'

'The cruel uncle will trouble the princess no more,' said the godmother. 'He broke his word to the witch and would not share his wealth with her and in revenge she made a magic circle round his castle and the ground opened and swallowed the castle and everyone in it. The witch, in her delight at seeing the earth shaking, missed her footing and stepped inside the circle and was lost.

The princess is now without parents or kindred, and it is for me to choose a husband for her, a husband who will be brave and kind. You have proved yourself to be both and I now offer you her hand in marriage.'

Art turned towards the princess, who said that of all the men she had ever met he was the one she would like to marry.

'There is one thing,' said Art.

'I know what is in your mind,' said the godmother. 'You are thinking of your mother.'

'Have no fear for her,' said the princess. 'She will be brought here and we will all live happily.'

Art and the princess were married and enjoyed many happy years together.

That was ages and ages ago and all these people have long since passed away.

The palace became empty and fell into decay. The sea came farther and farther inland. Nothing now remains on the beach where the palace stood but the beautiful colored stones and lovely shells which formed part of the Castle of Sleevebawn.

THE ENCHANTED LAKE

In olden times there lived in the northern part of Erin a chieftain named Conor. His wife had died when their little daughter Nessa was very young.

Nessa was the delight of her father's heart, for she grew into a beautiful girl and she was very good and gentle. Amongst her other gifts she had a lovely singing voice. So wonderful indeed was her voice that the birds often stopped their songs to listen to hers.

At a little distance from Conor's house there was a well which was believed to be bottomless. This was always covered with a large stone which was only removed when the people of the house went to draw water. Everyone was careful to replace the stone after taking out the water because it was believed that if this was not done, the well would rise up and cover all the neighbourhood.

One lovely spring day, Conor and his men went out hunting. The women of the house wandered through the fields and meadows, enjoying the bright sunshine.

Nessa remained in the house, finishing some needlework. After a time she became a little tired and felt thirsty. She took a vessel and went to the well to get a drink of the clear, cool water.

On a hawthorn bush close by, a thrush warbled among the fragrant blossoms. Nessa removed the stone from the well and took a drink. Her heart was gladdened by the beauty all around her and she began to sing in answer to the thrush's notes. The bird stopped but Nessa continued her song and forgot the stone.

Suddenly she heard a hissing sound close by and, looking round, she saw an enormous black eel in the centre of the water, and the water itself rising and covering the land on every side.

She felt herself being drawn down, down

into the depths of the dark lake. Then the eel rose with her to the surface and took her to the water's edge.

'I am the wizard of the lake,' said he, 'and you are now in my power. I will give you your choice, whether you will be drowned in the lake or have your legs changed into a fish's tail and live here in the water as a fish.'

'Oh,' said Nessa, 'I would prefer any fate to that of being drowned in that horrible lake.'

'Be it so,' said the eel, and immediately the poor girl's legs were changed into the tail of a fish.

'Now,' said the eel, 'you must live in the water. Part of the time you will spend in the lake, then you will pass through the river that flows out of it towards the north till you reach the open sea. You must leave the sea at midnight and return to the lake.'

'Will I never be able to look on the hills and trees again?' asked poor Nessa.

'You will. Each morning at sunrise, you may come to the surface of the lake and stay for a short time on the bank at the water's edge. When the sun has risen over that mountain on the east, you must again descend into the lake.'

'How long must I remain like this?' Nessa asked.

'As long as I live,' said the eel. 'If I were dead, you would be free from this spell and would get back your human form; but I will live for a long time indeed, for no one can kill me but a prince with a brown mole on his right hand and such a prince is not to be found in all Erin.'

Day after day, week after week, month after month, poor Nessa passed the dreary hours in moving to and fro from the lake, through the river, to the sea. Only for a short time at sunrise did she see the distant trees and hills.

Then her sad, sweet song rang over the still waters:

'Here must I stay,
By night and day,
If the prince with the strong brown hand,
Comes not here from a distant land,
The eel to slay.'

When the women returned from the fields,

they were terrified to see that the castle and grounds had disappeared and in their place was a great lake.

Everyone understood what had happened. It was known that Nessa had forgotten to replace the stone and that she was swallowed up in the rising waters.

When Conor heard the sad news, his grief was terrible to behold. He and all his followers fled from the dismal place and made their home many miles away. The chieftain mourned his daughter as dead. In his home there was no mirth nor joy. All was sad and lonely.

One day in spring, nearly a year after Nessa's disappearance, a traveller arrived at Conor's house. He was young and handsome and said he had come from a distant land.

With Irish hospitality Conor welcomed the stranger.

He asked his name.

'Donnlamh is my name,' said he.

'Why have you left your own country to come to visit ours?'

'Some of my ancestors came from Erin in days gone by, and I have heard so much of its beauty that I longed to visit such a lovely land.'

Conor renewed his words of welcome.

'There is another reason, too, for my desire to come to Erin,' continued Donnlamh. 'There is a wise old man in my father's court who came from Erin in his boyhood. He has the power of hearing strange and distant tidings. He hears voices in the winds and in the waves of the sea. He came to me one day and told me there was sorrow in Erin, on the northern shore at the river's mouth, for he had heard the moaning of the wave of Tuaidhe, which always means trouble and disaster.

'"Hasten to Erin," he said, "special work awaits you there, work which none but you can do."'

'We are very glad to have you here,' said Conor, 'but I am sorry you have not come to a happier home.'

He then told Donnlamh of the loss of his daughter and the full story of the well.

'I would like to see that lake,' Donnlamh said.

'It is the most desolate and deserted place

in Erin now,' replied Conor. 'It is believed to be completely under the power of a wicked wizard and no one will dare to go near it.'

Donnlamh made further enquiries about the distance and direction of the lake.

Next morning he was nowhere to be found.

He had left Conor's house before daybreak and set off for the far-off lake.

He had travelled a good distance when he came upon a boy standing by the roadside with a sling in his hand. The boy was fixing a stone in the sling to hurl at a bird in a tree nearby.

'Oh, don't kill the poor bird,' said Donnlamh.

'Here,' said he, handing the boy a gold coin, 'take this and give me the sling. It will be safer in my hand than in yours.'

The boy handed him the sling and went off, well pleased with his bargain. Donnlamh now began to feel hungry. After a short time, he came to a tiny house under a large ash tree. There was a stream near the house and bending over the stream was an old woman. She was trying to gather watercress but it grew at the far side of the stream and she could not reach it. Donnlamh got the cress for her.

The woman thanked him and asked him would he come into her house and rest awhile.

Donnlamh was glad to do this and enjoyed very much the oat cake and sweet milk which the woman gave him.

'Have you a long journey before you?' she asked.

'Yes, I have many miles yet to travel.'

'You have befriended me and for your kindness I will give you three gifts which will be useful to you.

'First, take this apple. It will satisfy your hunger at all times, for no matter how often you eat it, it will never get smaller but will continue to grow again.

'The second gift is this green pebble. If ever you or any of your friends are in danger, this pebble will prove to be a useful weapon.

'The third gift is my blessing; the widow's blessing which always brings luck.'

Donnlamh thanked the woman, and as he started off on his journey again, she stood at the door and blessed him till he was out of sight. He travelled on for many miles and began to feel very tired. Towards evening he came to a large blackthorn tree. There was an old man standing near it.

'Kind stranger,' said the man, 'will you take this knife and cut one of the branches for me? I am old and feeble and cannot walk without the aid of a stick.'

'I will, with pleasure,' said Donnlamh, as he climbed up the bank where the tree grew.

'Will you cut two sticks,' said the man, 'one for yourself and one for me?'

Donnlamh cut the two sticks.

'I will rest for a while,' said the man, 'and you can continue your journey. That stick will give strength, not only to you yourself but also to anyone who travels with you. It will make even the longest journey easy and pleasant.'

Donnlamh was astonished to find how much the stick helped him. He seemed to skim over the ground and all his weariness was gone.

He travelled on, and on, and at each step the way became more desolate and deserted.

Stillness and gloom reigned on every side. Day was beginning to break when he came in sight of a large spreading lake. As he went towards it, he saw on the bank at the edge what seemed to be a mass of bright shining gold. He drew nearer and there he saw a beautiful girl with her golden hair rippling round her. She did not see him, for she was looking into a mirror which she held in her left hand. With the other hand she was combing her flowing tresses.

All at once she began to sing.

Her voice was the sweetest and saddest Donnlamh had ever heard.

These words reached his ears:

'Here must I stay,

By night and day,

If the prince with the strong brown hand,

Comes not here from a distant land,

The eel to slay.'

Donnlamh at once knew he was the prince, for on his right hand was a large brown mole.

He answered in song:

He drew nearer and there he saw a beautiful girl with her golden hair rippling round her. She did not see him, for she was looking into a mirror which she held in her left hand. With the other hand she was combing her flowing tresses.

'Oh! maiden dear,
No longer fear,
The terrors of the lonely lake,
The strong brown hand the spell will break,
And help is near.'

Donnlamh and Nessa looked at each other in silence for a moment. Then Donnlamh said: 'You are Nessa, daughter of the great chieftain, Conor.'

'Yes,' replied the girl. 'Have you come from my father?'

'I have been to your father's home, but I came here of my own free will. Your father has told me the story of the lake. He believes you are dead.'

'Mine is almost a worse fate than death. I must remain here and in the sea as a mermaid unless a prince with a brown mole on his right hand comes here to slay the eel, which is the evil wizard of the lake.'

'A prince with a mole on his right hand?' asked Donnlamh.

'Yes,' Nessa replied, 'and such a prince is not to be found in Erin.'

'He must then, come from a distant

country?' Donnlamh said.

'Yes,' said Nessa sadly, 'if he ever comes.'

Donnlamh extended his right hand towards her, saying, 'He has already come, for I am he and Donnlamh is my name.'

'Oh!' cried Nessa. 'But how can you kill the eel? You have no sword nor spear nor any other weapon.'

Donnlamh remembered that he had the sling and the green pebble in his pocket.

'I have a weapon,' he said, 'which may be more powerful than sword or spear. When does the eel appear?'

'He will come to the surface very soon now. When the sun has risen over that high mountain to the east, he will take me again into the depths of the lake.'

Donnlamh crouched down behind the bank where the mermaid lay. He fitted the pebble into the sling.

Gradually the golden rays of the sun scattered the mountain mist.

A hissing sound was heard in the lake and the head of the eel appeared above the water.

Like a flash, Donnlamh hurled the pebble

and struck the eel with great force. A shriek rang out and then the lifeless form of the monster sank down into the water.

At the same time, Donnlamh saw Nessa coming towards him from the edge of the lake. She was dressed in a beautiful robe of sea green and had a diadem of pearls on her head. A girdle of tiny shining shells encircled her waist.

'How can I thank you?' she said.

'We will not talk of thanks till we reach your father's castle.'

'Alas!' exclaimed Nessa. 'Our old castle is now under the water of the lake.'

'You will be happy in your new house,' said Donnlamh, 'for it is the people, not the place, that make the home.'

'But where is my father's home?'

'Many miles from here but the journey will be neither tedious nor tiresome. Take my hand. This stick gives strength and support and shortens the way.'

Conor's delight knew no bounds when he saw his beloved daughter again. There was great rejoicing throughout the household. Everyone praised the young prince for his daring and courage.

'I hope you will make your home in Erin,' said Conor. 'We would be proud to have such a brave prince amongst us.'

'I would be happier in Erin than in any other place in the world,' said Donnlamh, 'especially if I could have your beautiful daughter for my wife.'

Nessa said she was more than willing to marry him.

The wedding took place almost immediately and never was there a happier pair in Erin nor in the wide world than the prince and his beautiful bride.

THE TREACHEROUS WATERS

'We cannot go on living as we are at present.'

'No, our riches are almost at an end.'
'You, Maeve, have been very extravagant.'

'Well, that is certainly the pot calling the kettle black. Think of the fortunes you have spent, your first wife's and mine.'

'It was easy to get through your fortune, Maeve, considering the amount of it.'

The speakers were a chieftain named Connla and Maeve, his second wife.

Connla's first wife had died when Clodagh, their only child was seventeen years old.

Connla did not long remain a widower. He married Maeve believing she was very rich. In reality she was very poor. She on her part thought he had great wealth.

They were both bitterly disappointed and were now facing poverty.

'I see only one solution for our difficulties,' said Maeve.

'What is your solution?'

'That Clodagh must marry a rich man.'

'A very good idea, Maeve. You are a clever woman. With her beauty and talents Clodagh should be able to find a rich husband and so bring wealth into the family.'

Just then they saw a carriage stop in front of the house.

An elderly man accompanied by an attendant came to the door.

The attendant spoke. 'One of the horses has lost a shoe,' said he. 'May this gentleman remain here while the animal is being shod?'

Maeve noticed the rich apparel of the stranger and the splendour of his carriage.

'We shall be pleased and honoured to have the gentleman as our guest,' was her answer.

'Having heard of the beauty of the

surroundings here I came to visit this part of the country,' said the stranger.

'May we know your name?' asked Connla.

'Eh! Eh! speak a little more loudly please. I am slightly deaf.'

Connla repeated the question in a much louder voice.

'Oh! Yes, Yes. My name is Angus and my home is Dunmore Castle.'

'I have heard of him,' whispered Maeve to her husband, 'he is a widower and one of the richest men in the country.'

Turning towards Angus she said: 'You are indeed very welcome.'

At that moment Clodagh came into the room.

She had been walking through the woods and had gathered bunches of primroses and violets.

Angus gazed at her in admiration.

'She is the impersonation of spring,' he thought.

'Clodagh,' said her father, 'this is the chieftain Angus. He has come to see the beauties of the country round here.'

'He is enormously rich,' whispered

Maeve, 'be as charming as you can.'

Clodagh after speaking a few words to the visitor retired to the farthest end of the room.

'You will please remain and have a meal with us,' said Maeve to their guest.

'I should indeed like to do so,' was the prompt reply.

While Connla and Angus were talking together Maeve told Clodagh she would like to speak to her.

'Do everything in your power,' she said, 'to entertain our visitor. Try to make him as happy as possible.'

Later on Maeve asked Angus if he would like to hear some music.

'Clodagh plays the harp and sings,' she said.

'Oh, I would indeed be charmed to listen to so fair a musician.'

Clodagh did as she was asked. As Angus watched her he began to feel how happy he would be to have such a beautiful girl as his wife to brighten his lonely life.

The evening wore on. Maeve declared that their guest could not possibly return home that night.

Angus was only too glad to remain. When he had retired for the night Connla and Maeve settled down for a chat.

Clodagh had gone to her own room.

'I am glad, Connla,' said Maeve, 'that we are alone. I wish to speak to you. Our visitor is a very rich man.'

'Yes,' said Connla, 'I believe his wealth is unbounded.'

'Did you notice the admiring glances he cast at your daughter?'

'Yes, he seemed to be greatly attracted by her beauty.'

'Now, Connla, we must make the most of things and bring about a marriage.'

'But, Maeve, I heard that he was very cruel to his first wife and that she died of a broken heart.'

'Nonsense, there is no such thing as a broken heart.'

'Listen now. We want wealth. Good fortune has given us the opportunity to find it. Clodagh must marry Angus.'

'I am sure she will refuse to marry him.'

'We will compel her.'

'Well, Maeve, I will leave the matter in your hands! You are a wise woman.'

'You are leaving it in good hands.'

Clodagh had a loyal friend in the person of Una, her foster mother.

Una was a widow. She lived with her son Feilim in a small house near Clodagh's home. There was great love between her and the lonely girl.

When all was quiet after the eventful day she stole out and went to Una's house.

When Una heard the knock she wondered who was the late visitor.

'Oh, come in *a' leanna*,' she said when she opened the door. 'I did not expect to see you so late in the night. Speak softly. I have a visitor in the house.'

'A visitor!' exclaimed Clodagh in surprise, 'who may I ask?'

'This morning Feilim was out in his boat. He saw another boat which had capsized.

'There was a man clinging to it. He was almost unconscious when Feilim reached him but he managed to get him ashore.

'Our house here was the nearest one to the place where he landed.

'With my help Feilim managed to bring him in. Come and look at him. He is still unconscious.'

As Una opened the door of the room, Clodagh looked at the still form lying on the bed.

'Oh! Una, will he recover?' she asked.

'He will, *a stór*. Look he is better already.'

The stranger opened his eyes for a moment and looked at the beautiful girl. Then he relapsed into unconsciousness.

'I wish I could stay, Una. But I must hurry back. No one knows I have left home. I hope the patient will soon recover.'

'It was well Feilim was so near,' said Una. 'Yes, indeed, both you and he have done much for the stranger. Good night, Una.'

'Good night, *a leanna*, and happy dreams.'

Early next morning Una went to look at the invalid. To her surprise she found him sitting up in bed.

'Tell me, please,' he said, 'where am I and what has happened?'

'You were brought here yesterday after having been taken from the sea.'

'I remember the boat capsized.'

'Yes, and Feilim, my son, was near by and managed to bring you ashore. Then with my help he brought you here.'

'The last thing I remember was my effort to cling to the upturned boat, but since I have lain here I have had a strange dream.'

'A dream?' said Una.

'Yes, and a very pleasant one. I saw a beautiful girl standing near the bed. Her eyes seemed to regard me with kindness and sympathy.'

'Perhaps you may see that beautiful face again.'

'Indeed I hope so, but how am I to thank you and your son for all you have done for me!'

'We need no thanks. You are welcome as the flowers of May.'

'I shall never forget your kindness, but I must return home. My people will be anxious about me. I am their only child.'

'Is your home far from here?'

'Not far if the voyage is made by sea, but a long distance by road past the Caraun lake.'

'Oh!' said Una, 'don't go by that lake. I would take the longest sea voyage rather than go near it.'

'You think the lake is enchanted.'

'I am sure it is. The water rises up suddenly and drowns everything near it for miles round.'

Just then Feilim came in. He was pleasantly surprised to see the visitor so far recovered.

'A safe uprising to you, *a chara*,' he said. The stranger clasped his hand.

'How can I thank you?' he said. 'You saved my life.'

'I am sure,' said Feilim, 'it is a life well worth saving. Now that I see you awake I know who you are. You are Ruairí, the son of Turloch and Aoife who live at Carraigbán Castle.'

'That is indeed who I am. I fear my parents will be anxious about me.'

'Feilim,' said Una, 'will you take the boat and go and tell Ruairí's parents that he is safe and well?'

'Yes, mother, but I will not be able to return home at once as the wind will be against me.'

Next day was a long dreary one for Clodagh. The greater part of it was spent in the company of the tiresome guest.

It was a relief to her when bedtime arrived and she went to her own room, but to her surprise she found her stepmother there.

'Now Clodagh, my dear,' said Maeve, 'you must be very bright and you must do all in your power to please Angus.

'Indeed I felt angry today you were so cold and dull. Wear your best dress tomorrow and be as pleasing and charming as possible.'

'Why should I try to please Angus? I do not even like him.'

'But you *must* like him. He intends to make you his wife. Your father and I have given our consent to a marriage.'

For a moment Clodagh was silent. Then with cold determination she said: 'A further consent is necessary and that is mine and my consent will never be given.'

Maeve had always found Clodagh gentle and even submissive. She was so much astonished at the answer she had received that she passed out of the room slamming the door behind her.

Just then Connla came to the door.

'Oh! I am glad you have come. I have been speaking to your stubborn daughter. She refuses to marry Angus.'

'Come back in with me. I may be able to persuade her.'

They both entered the room.

'Clodagh, my dear,' said Connla, 'I know you will be reasonable and do as we wish.'

'I will ask you a question, Father. If my mother were alive would she ask me to marry him?'

'Well, well,' Connia began.

'Now you old simpleton,' said Maeve, 'don't be sentimental. Remember, we are almost beggars.'

'Let the matter rest for the night,' said Connla, 'but I will ask you Clodagh to grant me a request. Angus is anxious to see the countryside. We are taking him for a drive tomorrow. He wished that you will come with us.'

'Give me time to think, Father. I am very tired. Please leave me to myself.'

'Very well, Clodagh. Come Maeve. If we keep her from sleeping she will not be able to accompany us tomorrow. Goodnight, my child.'

When left alone, Clodagh began to think how she could escape from the scheming of her stepmother.

'My loved foster mother will help me,' she thought.

Late as it was she set out for Una's house.

To her surprise she saw Ruairí sitting at the fire.

'Here,' said Una, 'is one who was anxious for your recovery.'

'Kindness seems to dwell in this neighbourhood,' said Ruairí. 'Mother, son and friend have all helped to bring me back to life.'

'I cannot claim any share in restoring your health,' said Clodagh.

'The sympathy in your kind glance has done much to give me strength and courage. I have seen your face in my dreams.'

After further talk Clodagh declared she must hurry home.

Una accompanied her part of the way. She told her all about Ruairí.

'I suppose he will soon return home!' said Clodagh.

'Somehow he does not seem to be in a hurry to go. Feilim and I love to have him in the house. I wish he would stay a good while.'

'So do I,' thought Clodagh.

Then she told Una of the wishes of her father and stepmother.

'They want to force me to marry old Angus,' she said. 'I hate to be in his company. They have planned that all four of us will go for a drive tomorrow morning. Can you think of any way that I could escape from going with them?'

'Let me think,' said Una. 'Yes, I believe I can help you.'

'Oh! Una you have always been my dearest and best friend.'

'Now listen, *a leanna*. Let us return to the house.

'There is a strange plant growing at the back. It is said it was brought here years and years ago by some foreign sailors. While outside it is not noticeable but when brought indoors the air becomes heavy. After a while everyone grows drowsy and gradually a deep sleep overcomes all present. Take some of

'Leave it outside your window till you are quite ready for sleep. Then take it in and sniff it. You will become drowsy. Throw the plant out the window and hurry into bed.'

this plant with you.'

'What shall I do with it?' asked Clodagh.

'Leave it outside your window till you are quite ready for sleep. Then take it in and sniff it. You will become drowsy. Throw the plant out the window and hurry into bed. Soon you will be in a heavy sleep which will last for many hours. It will be impossible to waken you until the effects of the plant wears off. That will be a very long time after you have fallen asleep. It will, of course, then be much too late for you to go for a drive.'

'Oh! Una, you are very good and clever.'

'Hurry home now *a stór*. Good night and good luck.'

Clodagh followed closely all the directions given by Una. She was soon in a sound, dreamless sleep.

Next morning Angus, as usual, breakfasted in bed.

'I must not delay,' he thought, 'I am looking forward to the drive with the beautiful Clodagh.'

When Connla and Maeve came down to breakfast they were much surprised to find that Clodagh was not in her usual place.

'Where is that troublesome girl?' asked Maeve.

'Perhaps,' said Connla, 'she was tired, better let her sleep awhile.'

'And keep the old man waiting! Not at all. I will go at once to her room and find the cause of the delay.'

Clodagh was in a deep sleep when Maeve entered the room.

'You lazy creature,' she exclaimed as she tried to waken her. She called her. She shook her. She pinched her.

All in vain. Clodagh slumbered on serenely. Maeve hurried back to Connla.

'I can't waken her,' she said, 'but she looks perfectly well and healthy.'

Connia glanced out the window.

'Oh! look,' he exclaimed. 'There is old Angus walking to and fro. I am sure he is impatient to be off. What are we to do? We dare not keep him waiting.'

'Oh, tell him Clodagh was very tired and was taking a rest. Say she wished to be bright and cheerful so that she could play and sing for him tonight.'

'Where is fair Clodagh?' asked Angus,

when the carriage was ready.

'She was very tired this morning and thought it better to rest awhile,' said Connla.

'Yes,' added Maeve, 'she was sorry to lose this opportunity of being in your company. She wished to rest so that she might be able to sing and play for you tonight.'

'Well, I suppose I must be content to wait for the evening to see the dear girl.'

'In what direction shall we go?' asked Connla.

'I would like to go to see the wonderful lake beside the mountain that rises from the Corann plain,' said Angus. 'Is it far from here?'

'No,' was Maeve's answer, 'but people say it is dangerous to go near the lake.'

'What danger is attached to it?'

'It is said that sometimes the water rises up suddenly and sucks in everything in the neighbourhood.'

'Oh,' said Angus, 'I am sure that is only a *pisreóg* [superstition] that gives it an added interest. We will go and see the wonderful lake. There is nothing like an adventure for keeping one young.'

Maeve whispered to her husband, 'Connla, don't you think it would take a great adventure to bring back his youth?'

'Well,' answered Connla, 'we had better please the old fellow.'

After travelling for some time they came in sight of the lake.

'Oh! let us dismount,' said Angus, 'we must have a close look at the wonderful water.'

The drivers of the carriage, Art and Shane, determined to remain where they were.

The other three walked on.

'How beautiful the lake is,' exclaimed Angus. 'What a pity it is that the lovely Clodagh is not with us.'

They continued walking till suddenly Connla called out, 'The lake is rising. Let us return.'

Then they felt that by some unseen power they were kept rooted to the spot on which they stood. Higher and nearer came the water till at last they found themselves drawn into the surging waves.

The drivers witnessed all this. They got

quickly into the carriage and hastened back to the castle.

Towards evening Clodagh wakened from her long sleep. She went at once to Una's house.

Ruairí and Una were standing at the door looking at the golden sun as it sank behind the mountains.

'Well, *a leanna*, had you pleasant dreams?' asked Una with a knowing smile.

'Indeed I did not dream at all and when I wakened I was glad to get out into the fresh air.

'You will think it strange,' she continued as she turned towards Ruairí, 'to hear me speak of sleeping in daytime.'

'I hope you have not been ill,' was his reply.

Both Clodagh and Una smiled but they had no time to answer as at that moment a carriage drove up to the door.

'This is my father's carriage,' said Clodagh, 'and these are his men, Art and Shane.'

'Oh! the lake, the lake,' cried Art who seemed to be much frightened and agitated.

Shane was more calm and self-possessed.

'Tell me,' said Clodagh, 'where are my father and the others?'

'We went in the direction of Corann Lake,' said Shane.

'Oh! the lake, the cruel lake,' Art repeated.

'Wait a while, Art,' said Una. 'Shane, will you tell us what happened?'

'When we came in sight of the lake the old gentleman said he would like to have a close view of it. The three got out of the carriage and walked towards the lake. We remained near the carriage.

'After a while even at the distance we were from the lake we saw the water rising quickly. In a short time the three were carried into the whirling waves. We hurried home as quickly as possible.'

'Oh! my poor father!' cried Clodagh.

'Your poor father!' thought Una, 'much he cared about you.'

Aloud she said: 'Let us all come into the house.'

'No,' said Shane, 'we must return to the castle, though for the future there will be no one living there.'

'Come in *a stór* and rest,' said Una, as she took the hand of the trembling girl.

Ruairí had gone for a long walk. On his return to the house he was astonished to hear of all that had happened. He felt very much for Clodagh but was at a loss as to how he should speak to her.

Just then Feilim came in.

'Mother,' he said, 'there are some important visitors coming here.'

'Who are they?' asked Una.

'I got directions not to mention who they are. They said they would announce themselves.'

Just then Ruairí uttered a cry of joy. 'My father and mother!'

'We planned to give you a surprise,' said Turloch, the father.

'And indeed a pleasant surprise it is,' said Ruairí.

Aoife, the mother, took Una's hand in hers as she said, 'How can we thank you for all you have done for our son?'

'It was a joy to have him here,' was Una's reply.

'Mother,' said Ruairí, 'Una, Feilim and Clodagh have been the kindest of friends to me.'

'Oh! I had no share in the kind hospitality,' said Clodagh.

'As I have said before, Clodagh, your sympathy has helped me much.'

Turloch and Aoife exchanged knowing glances. 'Clodagh is my foster child,' said Una, 'loved as if she were my very own.'

'I am sure, Clodagh,' Aoife said, 'the affection is fully returned.'

'Oh! Yes. I love Una very dearly,' was Clodagh's answer.

'The evening is turning a bit cold,' said Feilim as he piled some sods on the fire.

'Indeed,' Una said, 'there are holes in the roof and it is hard to keep the place warm.'

'You should have a better house,' Aoife said.

Seated round the fire they all heard and told everything that had happened.

Then Turloch spoke.

'We have brought two boats with us. The boatmen are in them. We want you all to come with us to Carraigbán and make your home there.'

'Oh! won't you come, Clodagh?' asked Aoife. 'One great desire of my heart will be fulfilled if you do. I have always longed for a daughter.'

'You will come, Clodagh,' said Una.

'But, Una, how can I be happy when I think of my father's fate?'

'There are no ties to hold you here and you should think of the happiness of others,' Una said.

Clodagh still hesitated.

'Do come, Clodagh,' whispered Ruairí.

These words put an end to all doubts.

The voyage to Carraigbán was very pleasant. The night was beautiful with the calm sea and the light of the full moon.

'Welcome home,' said Turloch as they reached the castle.

'Yes,' said Aoife, 'I hope it will be a happy home for all of us.'

It was a happy home for all. After some time there was a great wedding. Ruairí was the handsome bridegroom and Clodagh the beautiful bride.

'And as time passed away
They were happy and gay
For many and many years after
And their home was made bright
And filled with delight
By their children's gay frolics and laughter.'

THE JEWEL OF TRUTH

In a fine mansion on the Galway coast there lived, long ago, a rich man named Donal with Róisín, his wife, their two sons and their daughter Alva.

One day Donal and his two boys went out for a sail in their boat. When they did not return as soon as they had expected, mother and daughter became anxious.

Towards evening a message came to say that the boat had capsized and all were lost.

Róisín and Alva were overwhelmed with grief when the sad news was brought to them.

Their home was desolate. All joy and hope seemed to have departed from it.

Alva feared that her mother would never recover from the shock. She did all in her power to console and sustain her in her grief.

Both mother and daughter received much help and consolation from Orla, a kind woman who had been nurse to Róisín and afterwards to Alva.

Gradually Róisín became more calm but her health declined. Orla watched her with fear and anxiety.

Alva, too, began to see that her mother's days were numbered. Gloom and sorrow now loomed large in the poor girl's life.

With the loss of her loved ones the happy days seemed to be gone for ever.

At some distance from the mansion there lived a widow named Caitríona and Cathleen, her daughter.

They were not a happy pair. They were constantly squabbling and bickering. 'The Cats' was the name by which they were called in their neighbourhood, partly on account of their names and also for their continual quarrelling.

Before the death of her husband Caitríona had been well off, but both she and her daughter were very extravagant. Their wealth seemed to melt away and they found themselves very poor.

They were not a happy pair. They were constantly squabbling and bickering.

One day when they were talking about the future Cathleen said: 'You know, Mother, you have been very extravagant.'

'How dare you say that,' was the mother's reply. 'If I did get through our wealth it was because I spent it on clothes and jewels for you to hide your ugliness.'

'If I am ugly, Mother, it is from you I took my plain face and stodgy figure. My father was a handsome, well built man.'

For a moment there was silence between the angry pair.

Then the mother said, 'I see one faint ray of hope in all the darkness.'

'Oh! What is it?' asked Cathleen.

'My cousin, Róisín, is very ill. Indeed it is said she is not far from death. You know she is very rich.'

'Yes, her daughter will have everything she wants, not like me.'

'Be silent, girl, and let me speak. Róisín is very kind and generous. Perhaps if she knew how poor we are she might come to our aid.'

'Oh, Mother, I am sorry I was cross and ill-tempered. You are wonderfully clever. I knew you would find a way out of the trouble. Let us go at once to Róisín's house.'

Next day the pair set out on their journey. They found Róisín very ill.

'Now, Cathleen,' said the mother, when they were alone together, 'we must be very attentive to Róisín. She has not long to live. We must try to please her in every way so as to secure a good part of her wealth.'

'But surely, Mother, her daughter Alva will inherit all the riches.'

'Not if we are clever enough to make Róisín believe that we will love her daughter and take care of her. Besides this, you know that after Alva we are the next of kin.'

Poor Róisín found her cousin so kind and sympathetic she sent for her to come and have more conversation with her.

'Oh! Caitríona,' she said, 'my heart is broken thinking of how sad and lonely Alva will be when I am gone.'

'Don't worry about the girl, Róisín. I will be a loving mother to her and Cathleen a fond sister.'

'Oh! What a good thing it is that you have both come. My mind is easy now.'

Caitríona went from the room well

satisfied with the manner in which everything was arranged.

She had scarcely left when Orla came to see her beloved Róisín.

'I am glad you have come, Orla. Will you bring my poor child to me?' said the sad mother.

'I am here, Mother,' said Alva as she knelt by the bed.

'Now, my child and my faithful Orla, listen carefully to what I have to say. Caitríona and Cathleen will help you to look after the affairs of the castle.'

'A nice pair to do it,' thought Orla, but as she feared to disturb the poor patient she remained silent.

'I want to give you both very definite instructions about the jewels.'

'Indeed,' said Orla, 'they are very valuable.'

'Yes, and there is one far more precious than all the others. It is the golden minn [a kind of diadem]. It has magic powers. It has been in the family for centuries. One of my ancestors had communication with the fairies. He always showed respect and regard to their forts and dwellings. This minn is a magic gift which was bestowed on him by the "good people". It is known as the Jewel of Truth. If the wearer says anything untrue the minn presses heavily on the head and causes great pain. If not removed it will after a time be the cause of death.'

'Has it ever been worn by one who told a lie while wearing it?' asked Alva.

'No, it has always been worn by people of truth and honour. Keep it safely Alva. You are well worthy of such a treasure.'

At dawn next morning Róisín died.

For a short time the 'Cats' were very amiable, but gradually they began to show themselves in their true colours.

They took complete possession of the house and all the valuables including the jewels.

Alva soon found herself as a poor dependant in her own house. One by one the members of the household went away. They could not live with the pair of tyrants. At last no one remained in the castle with Alva but the faithful Orla.

In the end the girl herself was so unhappy

that she with Orla went to live in a small house at some distance from the castle.

Matters remained like this for some time till an event occurred which brought about a new order of things.

A castle in the neighbourhood of Alva's home had been vacant for some time.

One day Cathleen came to her mother in a state of great excitement.

'Oh! Mother,' she said, 'there is an occupant coming to the nearby castle. You know it has been vacant for some time.'

'Who is coming?' asked the mother.

'A young man named Oscar. I believe he is very handsome and better still he is very rich. He is an only child. His parents will arrive at the castle later on.'

'Well now, Cathleen, wear your richest robes and be sure you look your best.'

Shortly after this conversation Oscar arrived. As he was driving past Alva's old home she was standing at the gate looking wistfully at the flowers.

'What a lovely girl!' he thought, ' but what a sad face.'

Caitríona and her daughter made no

delay in calling on their new neighbour.

After a short conversation Oscar said: 'On the day of my arrival I saw a very beautiful girl standing near your house.'

'Oh,' said Caitríona quickly, 'I suppose it was one of the girls from the neighbourhood.'

'Some of the girls round here are rather good looking,' said Cathleen.

'You are not one of them,' thought Oscar. Aloud he said: 'This girl seemed to me to be very sad.'

To change the conversation Caitríona said: 'We came to thank you for the kind invitation to the ball which is to be held in your house.'

'I shall be glad,' said Oscar, 'to meet the people of the neighbourhood.'

The 'Cats' kept on a long conversation. It was with joy and relief that Oscar at last saw them depart.

A short time before that fixed for the ball Oscar went out walking one morning.

As he approached the little house where Alva now lived he saw her coming towards it.

She was carrying a vessel of water which

she had got from a nearby well. A big dog walked by her side.

'It seems strange,' thought Oscar, 'that a girl of such beauty and elegance can be so poor as to live in that small house.'

He longed to speak to her. For a moment he hesitated. Then he went towards the house.

'The day is very hot,' he said, 'will you give me a drink of the cool, spring water?'

The dog eyed the stranger but after a moment seemed to approve of him.

As Alva handed the drink Oscar noticed her beautiful hands. He would have liked to talk to her but she remained silent as he thanked her.

As he went on his way he kept wondering why such a noble handsome girl should live in such poor surroundings.

The ball was a wonderful affair. All the people for miles round were present.

The 'Cats', as they were called, were arrayed in great splendour. Both wore costly garments which really belonged to Alva. Jewels sparkled on their necks and hands.

'Be careful, Mother,' said Cathleen, 'to

place the minn properly on my head.'

'Never fear, my child, I will arrange it so as to cover the scraggy hair and bald patches.'

Oscar, as a duty, had to ask Cathleen to dance with him. Simpering and delighted she placed her hand on his arm.

When the dance was over he led her to a seat. He would gladly have left her but she motioned him to a place beside her. He could not very well refuse to sit down and talk to her, or rather let her talk to him.

He became tired of her chatter and scarcely knew how to answer her.

As he looked at her costly jewels he said:

'That is a very beautiful minn you are wearing.'

'I am glad you admire it,' was Cathleen's reply. 'It is my most precious possession. It has been in the family for years and now it belongs to me alone.'

The minn began to press on her head. She tried to forget the pain. She continued to talk. The pain increased. She rose up suddenly saying: 'I am not well.'

Then in her agony she called to her mother, 'Remove this thing from my head or

I shall die.' The minn was removed and there was her head revealed with all its scraggy hair and bald patches.

At this moment Orla entered the room. She was accompanied by many attendants who had lived in the castle when the rightful owners were there.

'Oh, listen for a moment,' she said, 'and hear all the wrong this pair have done. They are not the owners of the castle.'

'If we are not the owners we are the next of kin,' shouted Caitríona.

'You may be the next of kin but though you have banished the rightful owner she is still there to claim her possessions.'

As Orla made this declaration the 'Cats' hurried away.

Declan, who had been one of Alva's most faithful servants followed them. Others joined him. They took the minn and all the other precious jewels from the fleeing pair.

After the departure of the 'Cats', Oscar asked: 'And where is the rightful owner of the castle?'

'In a small house some distance from here,' was Orla's reply.

'She should be restored to her home at once,' said Oscar. 'Let us go and find her.'

When Oscar, Orla and their followers reached the cottage there was no trace of Alva.

After a time they saw coming towards them Bran, Alva's faithful dog.

He was followed by Declan leading Alva herself. The girl appeared to be almost unconscious. Orla and Declan led her into the house.

Then Declan gave an account of what had happened.

'Some time after the Cats had departed from the castle,' he said, 'Bran came tearing towards me barking furiously. He ran for a short space in the direction of the cottage, then back towards me. He repeated this movement and then I knew he wished me to follow him.'

'Did you find Alva in the cottage?' asked Orla. 'No, and Bran seemed anxious that we would not delay but would follow where he led. We arrived at the side of the great waterfall just in time.'

Here there were cries of horror from the listeners.

'The savage pair had dragged Alva from the cottage towards the fall. They were just about to hurl her into the whirling water when Bran and I arrived. As they quickly loosened their hold they both stumbled. They at once met the fate which they had planned for our beloved Alva.'

'I think, Orla,' whispered Oscar, 'we had better leave you alone with the poor weary girl. I will send the carriage to take her home.'

Next day Oscar called at Alva's house. He was delighted to see her looking well and happy.

After they had talked for some time Oscar said, 'My father and mother will arrive at my house tomorrow. I should like to bring them to see you.'

'Oh! I shall be delighted to meet them both,' was Alva's reply.

Next day the parents arrived. After they had seen the house and grounds the mother said, 'You certainly, my son, have a lovely residence here.'

'Yes, indeed,' said his father,' all you want now is a nice, young wife.'

'I have been thinking that you, Father and Mother, would be very happy here and that it is time I should make a home for myself.'

'But you cannot live alone,' said the mother.

'In fact,' said the father, 'it is time Oscar got married.'

'That is what I think myself, Father, always supposing that the girl whom I wish to marry will be willing to be my wife.'

'Then you have met the girl you wish to marry,' said the father.

'Yes, and if you and Mother come with me to her house tomorrow you will meet her too.'

Well, the result of all was that Oscar and Alva were married and lived happily ever after. They had many children.

Poor old Bran was beloved by the whole household. The first grief ever known in the happy home was on the day the dear old dog died. The children shed many tears and the parents themselves could not conceal their grief.

'But,' said Róisín, the eldest girl, 'he was very happy all his life for he knew how much we loved him.'

'Yes,' said the father, 'love is the great source of happiness.'

As the years went by the children spent much of their time in the home of their grandparents. In fact they did not know to which of the houses they really belonged for both were to them 'Home Sweet Home.'

THE MOUNTAIN WOLF

Long, long ago there lived among the mountains of Kerry a rich man named Brendan and his wife Clíona. They had three children, twin boys Ruairí and Fergus aged twelve years, and Brian aged ten.

One day in early autumn the children were in the garden with Sheila, their nurse. Sheila had been nurse to their mother.

The boys loved her and she loved them. Brian was her special favourite, because he was particularly gentle and kind to her.

'Tell us a story, please, Sheila,' said Ruairí.

'I think, boys, by this time you have heard all my stories.'

'But we like to hear them over again,' said Fergus.

'Well, what one will I tell you?'

The boys thought for a while. Then Brian

said, 'Tell the one about the wolf.'

'Indeed I thought you were all tired of that but if you wish me to tell it, here it is. You have heard of the poor, lonely widow who lives in the little house beside the mill?'

'Yes,' came the chorus.

'Well, there is a sad story about her only child, Fiachra.

'One evening as darkness was coming on, Fiachra was standing at the door of his house. An old hag came along. She was so strange looking, that Fiachra thought she could not belong to this world. Her black eyes glared at him. She drew back her large cloak and from under it a fierce wolf appeared. It snarled and growled. Fiachra was afraid it was about to attack him. He hit it with a stick which he had in his hand.

'The woman held back the wolf but turned to Fiachra and said, "Before the night falls you yourself will have the shape of the animal you would have hurt. You will never recover your own form, unless someone calls you by your name, Fiachra."

'A mist came over the boy's eyes. When it cleared both the hag and wolf had disappeared.

'The spell, however, fell on poor Fiachra. When his mother came to the door to bring him in, he was not there. All she could see in the gathering darkness was a wolf hurrying towards the forest.

'The only one who saw what had happened was an old crippled man who sat near the house. He could not rise from his chair to call for help. It was from him I heard the story.'

'Where is he now?' asked Fergus.

'The old man died some months ago.'

'Poor Fiachra!' said Brian.

'Yes, poor lad, he has never been seen since, and all the wolves have gone from the forest, except one, which seems to have escaped from the hunters.'

'And the mother never found her son?' said Fergus.

'No, never, and she is a very sad old woman living all alone.'

Just then a messenger came to say that the boys were to go to their mother. She wanted them to go with her to the heather field.

Mother and children walked about the field for some time.

'Oh! Look, Mother,' said Fergus. 'I have found a piece of white heather. That will bring me good luck.'

The mother laughed. 'Indeed, my boy, many people believe white heather brings good luck, but, white or purple, it is pleasant to see the heather bells stretching out over the field.'

Just then the mother uttered a sharp cry, 'Boys, there is a wasp's nest. Run from the field at once.'

The boys hurried out. The mother was the last to leave the field. A crowd of the wasps settled on her dress. When she reached home it was found she had been severely stung.

The doctor was sent for, but, by the time he arrived the poison had gone through her system. All kinds of remedies were tried, but the stings were so great and so numerous that poor Clíona lost the use of her limbs and it seemed as if she would never be able to walk again.

One day, about a year after the sad happening, the family were chatting together after lunch. Feilim, a man from the garden, came to tell them that Conn, the travelling man, had come to the house.

'Make him welcome,' said the father, 'the children love to hear his songs and stories.'

'May we go to him at once, Father?' asked Ruairí.

'Yes, of course. He will be as glad to see all of you as you will be to see him. I myself will come down later on. I wish your mother could come, too.'

'Don't trouble about me,' said the mother. 'I am happy when all of you are enjoying yourselves.'

When the boys went into the kitchen they found Conn sitting at the table having a good meal. It was a pleasant meeting.

'Welcome, Conn,' was the greeting from all three. 'It is more than a year since you were here before.'

'You must have a lot to tell,' said Ruairí.

'Well, I have some news but, before I begin to talk, tell me about your parents.'

'Father will soon be here to see you, but poor Mother cannot come,' said Fergus.

'I hope she is not ill,' said Conn.

The boys then told him all about the visit

to the heather field and its sad result.

When the father came in, the old man almost cried as he said: 'I am broken hearted to hear that the kind mother has had such ill luck.'

'I know how sorry you are, Conn. The home is not the same happy place since she became ill.'

'Can no cure be found for her?' Conn asked.

'No. We have had the cleverest doctors that can be found, but no one can cure her.'

The old man was silent for a moment. Then he said, 'Wasp stings sometimes resist all human skill but I would not despair. There is a rare bush that grows on the side of a mountain near the forest. It has large purple berries. The juice from these berries, when heated over a turf fire, is said to have wonderful healing power.'

'Could we possibly get these berries?' asked the father.

'Yes, but they must be collected by a relative of the patient.'

'Unfortunately,' said the father, 'I must leave home tonight and I will be absent for a couple of days, but I will try to get the berries immediately after I return.'

'Gathering the berries is not such an easy matter,' said Conn. 'There used be many wolves in the forest.'

'Yes,' said Ruairí, 'but I heard they are all gone except one.'

'That is true, my boy,' said Conn, 'but that one is very watchful, and it would be dangerous for anyone to go near him.'

'Well, Conn, we will see what can be done when I return,' said the father. 'Enjoy yourselves now, boys, while you have your friends with you.'

The boys spent a very happy evening with Conn. He sang songs, played games with them, and told them stories.

From birth the twins had always slept in the one room. Their beds, presses and everything were of the same pattern.

After saying goodnight to Conn they went to their room and settled down for a talk.

'I think, Fergus,' said Ruairí, 'that you and I should go to the mountain and try to get the berries that would cure Mother.'

'But what about the wolf?' asked Fergus.

'I have thought of that, but perhaps we could avoid him if we slipped out after dark.'

'How could we find the berries in the dark?'

'We could take a lantern with us.'

'Indeed, Ruairí, I would do anything to cure poor Mother.'

'Well, we will steal out tomorrow night.'

'All right, Ruairí. I won't be a bit afraid and I know you are as brave as a lion. We won't tell anyone we are going. I am sure we will be able to get the berries.'

Next morning Ruairí told Fergus that he was sure they would succeed in their attempt to get the berries.

'I was dreaming all night that I had killed the wolf,' he said.

'We had better bring hatchets with us,' said Fergus.

That night the two boys left the house while everyone thought they were in bed.

They went quickly to the mountain. 'Let us go round to the side where the berries are,' said Ruairí.

With the hatchets held firmly on their shoulders, they marched bravely on. Just as they reached the bush they heard a snarl and, on looking towards the forest, they saw the wolf glaring at them.

At the sight, terror seized them. They dropped their hatchets and ran for their lives.

They had not been missed, but the next morning there was great wonder among the workmen at the disappearance of the hatchets.

They told Brian of their adventure but warned him to keep it a secret.

Later in the day Brian was talking to Sheila.

'Conn has told us,' he said, 'that there are berries growing on the mountain that would cure Mother. All the wolves are gone from the forest except one. I wonder, Sheila, would that one be Fiachra?'

'Well, *a leanna*,' said Sheila, 'if there was someone brave enough to go to the mountain and call out the name Fiachra, we would know if the boy is there in the form of a wolf.'

Brian thought things over. He determined to go to the mountain and call out the name.

When he reached the mountain he heard a snarl and saw the wolf coming out of the forest. He was terrified.

That night Brian, instead of going to his room, slipped out quietly. He took the lantern with him.

When he reached the mountain he heard a snarl and saw the wolf coming out of the forest. He was terrified. His instinct was to run, but instead he called out the name, Fiachra.

Then in fear and terror he fell to the ground in a faint.

When he regained consciousness he saw a kindly face bending over him.

Two gentle arms helped to lift him to his feet.

'Oh! Who are you?' asked Brian.

'I am Fiachra,' was the reply.

'You have been under a cruel spell.'

'And you have broken the spell. When you called the name Fiachra, the form and nature of the wolf disappeared, and I can now go home to my poor mother.'

'You will have a happy meeting.'

'Yes, and I may thank you for our happiness. But why did you come here?'

'I was told there were berries on a bush which grows on the side of the mountain.

These berries are said to be a cure for wasp stings. Do you know where the bush is?'

'We will walk round the mountain and look,' said Fiachra.

When the boys found the bush, Brian wondered how he could bring the berries home.

He had forgotten to bring something in which to hold them.

'I have an idea,' said Fiachra. 'There is a tree in the forest that has enormous broad leaves. You can carry the berries on them.'

'While you, Fiachra, are getting the leaves I will begin to gather the berries. They must be gathered by someone who is related to the sufferer.'

With happy hearts the boys set out for home. When they reached Brian's house they parted, promising to meet again to talk over their wonderful adventure.

It was late when Fiachra reached his home. His mother was sleeping near a window which looked out on the street.

Fiachra tapped at the window and said softly, 'Mother.'

The mother turned in her sleep but did

not waken.

Again Fiachra knocked and called.

This time the mother sat up in bed.

'That was a strange dream,' she thought. 'I was sure I heard Fiachra's voice.'

Again Fiachra knocked and called. This time the mother pulled back the curtain. Then she gave a cry and almost fainted.

'Mother,' cried Fiachra, 'open the door. Your own boy is home to you again.'

It would be difficult to describe the delight of the pair.

Fiachra was from that day the joy of his mother's heart and her strength and comfort in her old age.

In the meantime Brian knew that there would be someone in the kitchen till a late hour.

He left the berries outside the door and went in. He found Conn and Sheila sitting at the fire having a great chat.

'Oh! *a mhic*, I thought you were in bed hours ago.'

'Hush, Sheila. I have something to show to you and Conn.'

He brought in the berries.

'These are the berries from the bush on the mountain,' said Conn.

'Yes, Conn.'

'How did you manage to get them?'

'I will tell you later on, Conn, but will you show me how they are to be used to cure Mother?'

Conn turned to Sheila and said, 'Get a three-legged pot, a little water from the well outside under the ash tree, and stew the berries over a turf fire.'

After some time, Conn said, 'Now put the juice into a basin and go and bathe the patient's feet.'

'Hurry, hurry, Sheila,' said Brian. 'We three will now go to Mother's room.'

Sheila was the first to enter the room. The mother was sitting at the fire, reading.

'Now, *a chuisle*,' said Sheila, 'it is time for you to be resting. I will bathe your feet and then you can go to bed.'

When Clíona put her feet into the basin she uttered a cry.

'Oh! What kind of water is this?' she said. 'My feet feel as they did before they lost their power.'

To her great joy she soon found she could walk again.

'What wonderful thing has brought about this cure?'

'Your son Brian may be thanked for it all. It was he who went to the forest and collected the berries which were the magic cure,' said Sheila proudly.

'But, Mother,' said Brian, 'it was Conn who told us about the berries.'

'That is true,' said Sheila, 'but you must tell your mother how brave you were going to the mountain to face the fierce wolf.'

'But, Mother, Ruairí and Fergus went to the mountain, too, but they did not know what Sheila had told me.'

Sheila then gave an account of poor Fiachra's transformation.

'Well,' said Clíona, 'there are two very happy mothers tonight, myself and Fiachra's.

'Our suffering is now turned into great happiness. Indeed it was by the helpful knowledge and advice of Sheila and Conn that everything has come right.'

A PRINCE IN DISGUISE

Prince Cormac was the only child of King Oriel and Queen Aoife.

The great desire of the parents' hearts was to see their son happily married. They determined to speak to him about choosing a wife.

'Cormac,' said the king, 'you must marry. Surely you will not allow the throne to descend to a stranger.'

'And,' added the queen, 'our great possessions to pass out of the family.'

'But, Mother, I am content as I am. Where could I find a wife I would love as I love you? And where could I find one with such beautiful raven hair and sparkling eyes as yours?'

'You, yourself, Cormac, have inherited

your mother's beautiful eyes and hair,' said the king.

Cormac possessed many natural gifts. He was handsome and brave and had won the affection of his people by his kindness and charm.

Among his many manly qualities was his skill as an athlete. He was almost tired of receiving homage and praise for his achivements on the sports field.

'Fergal,' he said one day to his best friend, 'it is because I am the prince that such great tribute is paid to my athletic triumphs.'

'Nonsense,' said Fergal, 'the applause is thoroughly deserved.'

'Well, I intend to put the sincerity to the test. I want you to help me to disguise myself and I shall play as an ordinary hurler.'

'And how will you arrange all that?'

'The players will be waiting for the arrival of the prince and when he does not appear I in my disguise will offer to fill the vacant place so that the game may be played.'

'Well, you have always enjoyed jokes and pranks. I hope this one will turn out to your satisfaction.'

The day for the contest arrived. The players on both sides were ready for the game, but where was the prince?

'The match must proceed,' said the captain on one side.

'Yes,' agreed the other captain. 'It would be unlucky to postpone it. It must be played today for the new moon will appear tonight and our matches are timed for the first appearance of the new moon.'

At this point in the conversation Cormac, wearing a wig and cleverly disguised, came forward and spoke in a foreign language. Fergal answered him in the same language.

'The game may go on as usual,' he said, 'if this player is allowed to take the vacant place.'

'By all means he will be allowed to play,' said one of the captains.

'And indeed,' said the captain on the other side, we are all very thankful to him for enabling us to proceed with the game.'

Opposite the ground where the match was to be played there was a beautiful castle. It had belonged to a chieftain named Niall who had lived there with Maeve his wife and their daughter Etain.

Maeve had died and after some years Niall had married a widow named Sorcha who had a daughter, Gráinne.

The second wife seemed at first to be very kind.

'I will be a mother to Etain, your dear child,' she said, 'and though Gráinne is some years older than your daughter they will love each other like sisters.'

There is a proverb in Irish which says 'Time is a good storyteller.' It had a sad story to tell about poor Etain. Her father died.

After his death Sorcha and Gráinne showed themselves in their true colours. They were very cruel to Etain. Gráinne hated her.

'Mother,' she would say, 'how is it that Etain looks more beautiful in her old clothes than I do in all my grandeur?'

'Never mind, my dear. We will keep her out of the way and no one will ever know how beautiful she is.'

Poor Etain had a very unhappy life.

Sorcha and Gráinne were among the spectators at the great match. From a small hillock on the side of the field they watched the play.

Etain longed to see the game. She managed to steal out of the house and got a place among the crowd. Like all the onlookers her eyes were fixed in admiration on one of the players who outshone all the others. His movements were swift and accurate and it might be said that the game centred round him.

Suddenly a ball whizzed towards him. There was a wail from the crowd as it struck him. He fell to the ground just near the place where Etain stood.

In her excitement she rushed towards him and raised his head. As she did so the fair wig fell away and the black, curling hair was revealed.

'Prince Cormac, Prince Cormac,' came the shout from the crowd.

For a moment Cormac opened his eyes and gazed at the fair face bending over him. Then he became unconscious.

'Let the prince be brought to my house,' said Sorcha, 'and send at once for medical aid.'

In her excitement she rushed towards him and raised his head. As she did so the fair wig fell away and the black, curling hair was revealed.

To the joy of all concerned the doctor said the injury was not serious. Rest and quiet were all that were necessary for complete recovery.

Sorcha and Gráinne were delighted to have the prince for their guest.

'Dress in your finest clothes, my daughter, and sing your sweetest songs,' said Sorcha. 'Do your best to charm and entertain the prince.'

Now Cormac was particularly musical. The harsh, out-of-tune singing that he was forced to listen to nearly drove him mad. News of the accident had, of course, been sent to the palace.

The king was absent from home when the message arrived but the queen set out at once to go to her son.

There was much delay on the journey. A rain storm had come on and travelling was very difficult. Shortly before the end of the journey the weather changed and the sun shone brightly.

As the carriages approached the castle, beautiful singing was heard from inside the orchard.

Stop the carriages for a while,' ordered the queen.

The singing ceased but out from the orchard came a lovely girl. Her fair hair had come loose and had fallen on her shoulders like a golden fleece.

The queen could not restrain her admiration.

'Fair maiden, what is your name?' she asked.

'Etain is my name, your Majesty.' Just then a huge, tall man came running towards Etain.

'Hurry, hurry, *a stór*,' he said. 'Your stepmother is calling and you know the sort of temper she has.'

When Queen Aoife reached the castle Sorcha and Gráinne went down on their knees to welcome her.

'I am thankful,' said the queen, 'for the hospitality and kindness you have shown to the prince, my son.'

'Oh, your Majesty, it has been a privilege and an honour to have him with us.'

The prince was delighted to see his mother.

After some time the queen said, 'As we were passing the orchard I heard most beautiful singing.'

'It must have been Gráinne, my daughter, your Majesty heard,' said Sorcha. 'She has a wonderful voice.'

'Yes, Mother,' said Cormac with a slight wink, 'she has indeed *quite* a wonderful voice.'

'When we reached the entrance to the orchard a lovely girl came out. I thought perhaps she was the singer,' said the queen.

'Oh! Not at all,' said Gráinne, 'she was merely one of the servants.'

'Though she was poorly dressed,' said the queen, 'she looked very beautiful with the sunshine gleaming on her golden hair.'

'Mother!' exclaimed Cormac, 'I have seen a girl like that in my dreams.'

'Your Majesty,' said Sorcha, 'the prince has been delirious nearly all the time since the accident. Nothing soothes him but a drink which I prepare for him.'

Cormac looked at the queen and said, 'Is it not strange, Mother, that I feel bright and strong till I take the drink? After having it I become dull and listless.'

The queen turned to Sorcha, saying, 'Thank you for your hospitality and kindness, which I hope to repay. I shall have arrangements made to take the prince home as soon as possible.'

The queen departed but soon returned to take Cormac home.

Sorcha and Gráinne were determined that neither Cormac nor the queen would see Etain. They had the girl locked in a room at the top of the house. No one was allowed to go near her.

There was only one person in the household who dared to befriend Etain. This was poor, simple Conn, who did most of the slavish work round the kitchens. He was a huge, strong fellow, but for all his size and strength he was very gentle and kind. All the animals round the house loved and trusted him.

Conn had a great affection for Etain. She told him all her troubles.

Very shortly before the departure of the queen and Cormac, Conn rushed upstairs to the locked room.

'Are you there, my girl?' he asked through the keyhole.

'Yes, Conn,' came the reply.

Conn hurled his great body against the door. The lock broke and he was soon in the room.

'Come quickly, *a stór*. They are all getting ready for the journey. We will slip out by the back door.'

Etain followed Conn. Before long they were out on the road.

The moon was shining brightly.

'Now,' said Conn, 'when we come to the orchard gate stand still. Leave the rest to me.'

Queen Aoife, Cormac and their retinue left the castle to the great disappointment of Sorcha and her daughter.

When the carriages were approaching the orchard, Conn rushed in front of them waving his hands.

'Stop, stop,' he said. 'Look towards the orchard gate.'

All eyes turned to where Etain stood in the moonlight. Her beautiful hair stirred lightly in the faint breeze.

'Mother,' exclaimed Cormac, 'that is the face I have seen in my dreams.'

Conn came to the carriage door.

'Oh, Queen,' he said, 'take pity on a poor, tortured girl and save her from the cruelty of a heartless pair.'

'Mother,' said Cormac, 'please take the girl into the carriage.'

'Oh,' said Etain, 'I cannot go without Conn, my best friend.'

'There is room for all,' said the queen. Etain remained silent after she had told why and how she had escaped from the castle.

Not so Conn.

'Won't there be hunger and thirst in the castle tonight?' he said, chuckling and rubbing his hands.

'You know, your Majesty,' he continued, 'Sorcha and her ugly daughter have fine appetites and like a good meal.'

'And will they not have one tonight?' asked Cormac.

Conn shook with laughter as he said, 'Hardly, your Highness. I collected all the hungry cats I could find and shut them in the pantries. How will it be when the cooks go to look for the milk, cream, beef, fish and all the good things that the cruel pair will be expecting for their evening meal?'

Not one of the company could refrain from joining in the hearty laughter.

The end of the story was that King Oriel and his queen got their wish when their valiant son was married to beautiful Etain.